Siad

of SOMALIA

BY THE PRISM AWARD WINNER

HARVEY SMITH

THE KIDS NETWORD®

Published by The Kids Netword®
1235 Williams Parkway East
P.O. Box 68532
Brampton, Ontario
L6S 4S0

PRINTED IN CANADA

**Canadian Cataloguing in
Publication Data**
Smith, Harvey, W., 1981-
  Siad of Somalia
(The Kids Netword series)
Published also in French under title:
Siad de Somalie

ISBN 0-929137-46-9

1. Somalia - Juvenile fiction.
I. Armstrong, Elaine. II. Title.
III. Series

Ps8587.M537S52 1997
jC813254C97-932136-0

PZ7.S649135Si 1997

Photographs courtesy of the Canadian Department of National Defence,
Ottawa, Canada

Special thanks to publishing partner, ITP Nelson Canada

Design by Peggy Rhodes

I⬤P Nelson

DEDICATED TO CAPTAIN BRIAN GRAY,

CAPTAIN PATRICK KOCH, AND ALL UNITED

NATIONS PEACEKEEPERS WHO HAVE WORKED

AND CONTINUE TO WORK FOR PEACE IN

SOMALIA AND AROUND THE WORLD

AND TO

THE PRISM AWARD JUDGES WHO CHOSE MY

STORY IN THE WAR AND PEACE CATEGORY.

PAUL, LESLY AND JUDITH

CHAPTER ONE

From Canada to Africa, December 1992

Private Merrick Flynn joined his comrades on deck and looked toward the horizon in the direction of Kenya, Africa. The journey that had begun with goodbyes to his family and friends in Halifax was finally coming to an end.

Many things were still uncertain to these Canadian soldiers as they stood in small groups on the deck and looked upon the strange new land before them. Duties would be assigned when they eventually arrived in Mogadishu, Somalia. Many of the soldiers were anxious to know more about the current conditions in Mogadishu. There were conversations about the fighting between the Somali warlords, the severe drought that had ravaged Africa, the media coverage of the starving Somalis, and the effort to secure Mogadishu harbour so that the U.N. relief workers could effectively distribute food supplies.

"Hey Flynn, ever been to Africa before?" one soldier asked with a nervous smile. "Parsons over there says some Yankee soldier-friend told him that

the snakes and spiders in our area of duty are poison-ous."

Private Flynn smiled back at his friend. Spiders and snakes were natural threats...the gunfire between fighting factions of Somali warlords would be anything but natural, and twice as deadly.

"No, I've never been to Africa," Flynn replied. "This should be quite an experience. The air is hotter than I imagined, even at sea."

"Yes, it's hard to believe it's December."

Private Flynn picked up his gear and headed toward the army jeeps waiting near the dock. This convoy was headed to the airport in Nairobi, Kenya where they would ship out immediately to an abandoned Soviet airfield just outside Mogadishu. He was tired, but he looked out as the convoy headed down the tree-lined streets and was surprised to see the many modern buildings that flashed by. He smiled as he remembered his mother's final words to him. "Take care, son," she had said as she bravely fought

tears. "Stay away from those wild African beasts and try to eat well." He knew his family would worry. He planned to send word of his safe arrival once he reached Mogadishu and learned more about his duties there.

CHAPTER TWO

Siad...
A Somali Child

Siad rubbed his brown eyes wearily and looked at the huge crowd. The mob was continually growing larger and larger. In a few minutes, thousands of people, including many of Siad's clan, would be lined up neatly...by Somali guards wielding M-16 machine guns. Ever since food supplies from far off countries had gotten through, the crowd of people in line to receive the day's only ration of brown gruel had kept growing. Siad was afraid. He clung to his mother and his two year old brother Sayyid. He knew the guns were dangerous and that they made a deafening noise. He had also

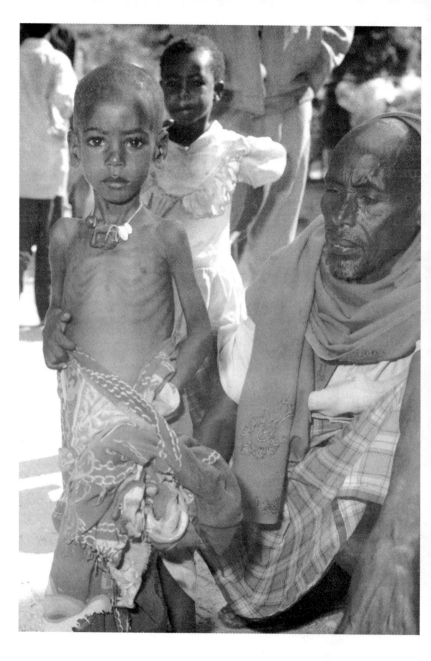

seen the guards cruelly strike people surging toward the food pots. Food had become scarce even before the latest fighting started. Siad could not remember the last time it rained. A few times, before they arrived at this camp, there had been a light mist that renewed their hope.

If only the rain would return and with it fresh water for the rapidly drying wells and parched riverbeds and pasture for their few remaining camels. If only the fighting was over, and things could go back the way they were, traveling the countryside with family, friends, and animals.

However, the rains never came, and they had to keep moving to find water. In their last stop before Mogadishu, the people left quickly because one of the warlords had ordered the village's only well poisoned. The remaining camels had been shot by mercenaries, hacked to pieces and thrown into the well. No one really knew why the warlord had done this. Many suspected that he thought the clans of nomads in the village were associated with a rival warlord. Siad knew the terror of having to run. He also knew hunger and death. Already he had lost a sister and one brother to starvation. Death came quickly and often to Siad's world.

Siad could remember the day his father had gone to fight for one of the warlords who opposed the Somali president. He understood that his father felt he must do this because the people were unhappy with many of the rules and decisions made by the president. With so much fighting, fear, confusion and hunger, Siad knew that this war was not going to help anyone.

He no longer knew where his father was, or even if he was alive. It seemed to Siad that his situation grew steadily worse. He was always hungry... his stomach bloated. He looked around him at the growing throng of people, some familiar, most of them strangers from many different areas who had sought refuge here. They fared no better. Nomads in long, black shawls who had joined with his clan as they fled to Mogadishu were so thin they appeared almost translucent. Huddled in a corner were children in makeshift shirts. Their hair was filled with red dust. Some of their parents had been killed in the fighting. These children were often neglected unless they had other clan members who would take care of them. Charity was scarce in the camps where feeding and caring for one's own self was often difficult.

The warlords who fought each other to control the country had split the people into separate fighting factions. Clans associated with one warlord learned to hate or even fight those associated with his enemies. This land that had searched for years for a sense of national identity was torn more than ever.

Boys Siad's age learned to wield deadly machine guns against each other in the struggle to live, often killing for food but sometimes to settle disputes among themselves or among rival clans. Their eyes were glassy and their minds dazed from chewing khat, an amphetamine-like drug that was commonly used by Somali men and boys.

These thugs were usually the only ones who ate on a regular basis.

People who could not defend themselves lived in fear, as the ones who presented the easiest targets were almost guaranteed to have their lives and the little food they had taken in this depraved society.

Sayyid soon began coughing violently, and Siad's attentions turned to his mother's attempts to soothe and comfort him. Siad wished they did not have to wait so long for their food. There were many children among the crowd who were not able to stand in line as Siad could. Diseases like pneumonia, dysentery, and illnesses associated with malnutrition were common. There were nurses from the Red Cross who tried to feed and tend to the sickest of the children. Siad admired their tireless efforts, but often food and medical supplies were slow to arrive or completely stopped as the warlords fought to control

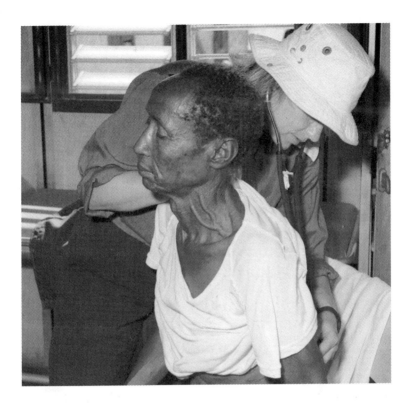

the city of Mogadishu, whose harbour and airfields were the lifelines by which the people of that area were kept from starvation. Several nights ago, there had been a raid on this food compound and Siad

sensed fear among many of the adults that this could happen again soon.

Suddenly the rusty iron gates swung open with an awful grating sound, and hordes of people surged through into the open courtyard where there were vats filled with hot gruel. The guards ran boldly amongst this living tidal wave, viciously whacking several women with sticks to restore order. Siad's mother took him by the hand and, with her two year old son in her arms, began to run through the crowd toward their goal, the food that would sustain them for another day. Quickly, a guard stepped in front of them and whacked Siad's mother hard on the shoulder. Her face contorted into a grimace of pain as her brittle arm began to swell. Siad knew the whack was a nasty one, and he felt like screaming but she silenced him.

"No, Siad. We will get our food soon," she said in Somali. Knowing they could advance no further, Siad's mother sat with the thousands of others in neat rows, kept in line by the Somali guards. If they were lucky, there would be enough food when it came time for them to approach. It was still early in the morning. Perhaps they could get their food and find a sheltered place to eat before the merciless noonday heat could torment them.

As they neared the front of the line, Siad

clutched his hollow gourd anxiously. The crowd had been large; would there be enough to feed his family? It was now mid-morning, and the sun had been up for several hours. By noon, it would beat down upon them ruthlessly. Siad feared that most of the shady spots would be already taken by the time they could leave the courtyard. Shelter from the sun was as difficult to get as food and water.

Siad was only twelve years old and not that strong, but he wished he could give his mother a rest from carrying the weakened Sayyid. His brother was hot and panting deeply. He knew some of his mother's anguish as she looked worriedly at the child from time to time. She had lost a daughter recently with pneumonia and severe dysentery. Another child had been stillborn, resulting from her own malnutrition and harsh lifestyle. Siad had heard her speaking with several other women and he realized her feelings of helplessness in not being able to care for her children. Sayyid had had diarrhea for several days and his

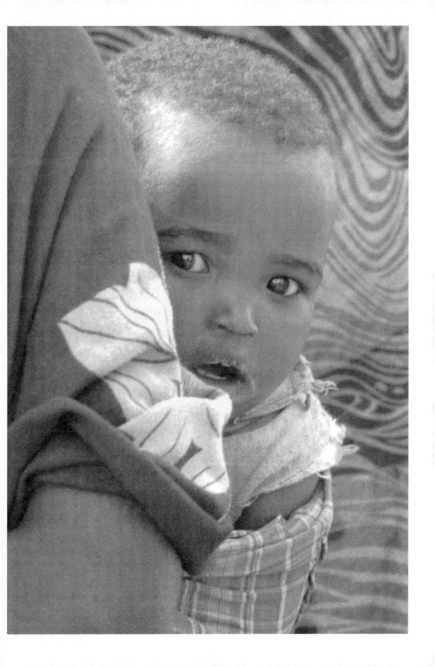

mother was afraid. Even now, she noticed several other women glancing at Sayyid and speaking softly of his weakened condition.

Finally, they reached the front of the line. It seemed like a dream to Siad. The smell of the food tantalized him as they neared the large vats. At last the wait was over, and they could escape the grim, prison-like courtyard, if only until the next day. Siad watched as the cook quickly scooped up some of the brown Unimix, a mixture of corn, beans, and vegetable oil, into hollow gourds for each of the children. As soon as his mother's small pot was filled, they fled the courtyard as swiftly as they could, desperately seeking shelter from the heat. To their relief, they found shade beside an abandoned hut and sat wearily with a few others. Siad wanted to eat immediately, but he knew he must wait for the gruel to cool. He had burned his hands, lips, and face before, when he had been too hasty to eat the scalding Unimix. As soon as it cooled, he devoured it, knowing it was his only meal for the day. Tomorrow, they would eat again if the warlords did not send their henchmen to raid the station and the food could get through to this area. He helped his mother feed Sayyid and settle him in the shade to sleep.

Later that afternoon, a nurse approached Siad and his mother. There was a small group of children with the nurse. Siad recognized one of them as Mohammed, the son of his father's brother, and one of his clan. The nurse smiled reassuringly and asked Siad to go with them. He promised medicine, but Siad was uncertain. He did not want to leave his mother. He watched curiously as the nurse examined the sleeping Sayyid and placed a red bracelet on the child's arm. The nurse spoke to Siad's mother in a concerned, hushed tone. After several minutes, Siad's mother spoke to him.

"Go, Siad. I want this nurse to help you. You will be alright. See? Look at Mohammed with the other children." Siad was still a little reluctant, but he took his place beside Mohammed as they were led to a small clearing. Each severely undernourished child got a spoonful of anti-diarrhea medicine. Then, each child was given a red or blue bracelet, depending on the seriousness of their condition. Siad's bracelet had to be drawn tightly around his thin, bony wrist. Although he had a bloated belly, Siad's limbs were extremely thin and flimsy. His lanky look was exaggerated because he was tall for his age. He smiled

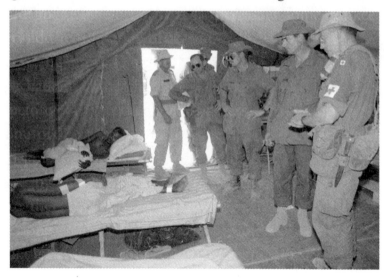

faintly as he thought to himself that his blue bracelet was the same colour as his blue shorts, although they were faded, torn in some places and mended in others. Siad and Mohammed giggled and showed each other their blue bracelets. The children were told to keep wearing them, and that from now on they would receive a protein biscuit with their daily ration. Siad and Mohammed smiled at each other and returned to find their parents.

CHAPTER THREE

In Deep Despair

The evening was approaching, and Siad, with his mother and baby brother, began searching for a suitable place to sleep. They wanted to be as close to the food compound as possible to avoid a long walk in the morning sun and a long wait in the line. They found a cool spot under a shady tree. As they settled for the night, Siad noticed Mohammed, who was with his father, also settling for the night. Mohammed's father had been sick and still looked very weak. Siad recalled earlier times when his own father, Mohammed's father, and the other men of the clan would gather around the night-time fire to sing songs, tell stories, and recite wonderful poems about horses, camels, love, and war. Siad, Mohammed, and the other boys from the clan would listen and try to take part. Their fathers had told them they must learn these ways in order to teach their own children the ways of their people. Siad loved these times. They were happy times and he longed for their return. The sound of the crowd and the swaying of his mother as she rocked the crying Sayyid began to lull him to sleep. Tonight there were no blazing fires, no songs or poems.

The next morning, when the iron gates of the courtyard were pushed aside, the crowd was again large and eager. This time, Siad's mother crept through the crowd slowly and silently. Today, the guard did not strike her, however, she was pushed and jostled as several others surged ahead. It was just before noon when they finally had their rations. When they left the courtyard, they discovered that the shadiest and most sheltered places to eat and rest were taken. After an hour wandering in the sun, Sayyid became sick and vomited. Siad was tired and sick and afraid. As they finally sat down, still unprotected from the sun, Siad cried silently and helplessly until no more tears came. He was so hot he thought he felt his skin blistering. He was dizzy, weak, and nauseous. He breathed rapidly and shallowly. Every day brought more people in search of food, water, and shelter. So many people... so little food... so much sickness... so much death.

In the cool of the evening, Sayyid slipped into unconsciousness. Siad seemed to settle into a deep sleep that was somewhere between consciousness and oblivion. When he was able to rouse himself from this state, he discovered that his mother was crying pitifully and rocking his little brother. It was a scene that Siad knew, but had forever been dreading. His little brother Sayyid was dead. Siad began to weep and sat huddled beside his mother. He slept in brief intervals through the night. Each time that he woke, his mother still rocked the tiny body of Sayyid.

The next morning, an eerie old man, his back hunched and twisted from some childhood disease, took Sayyid's body away. He was the area's undertaker. Siad had seen him collect bodies before. He also knew well where his brother would be taken. He had seen the large, open graves where bodies were placed daily, without ceremony or sympathy. Death was regarded by some as an escape from the hardship of living in anarchy and starvation. Others thought that all people victimized by the chaos in Somalia were doomed to die an early, painful, horrible death.

Siad hardly recognized his mother. She was sick with grief and her dark eyes were bloodshot from her constant crying and lack of sleep. Her long, flowing, dress-like garment was dirty and its once brilliant red colour had faded. She was still young, but the youth and beauty had faded from her face. Her cheeks seemed hollow and her skin had become lined and wrinkled. Her body was weakened from her long hours in the heat with little food or water. Siad found that she was too weak to stand without assistance.

He had never known such despair and hopelessness.

He missed his little brother, the fate of his father was unknown, and he feared that his mother would die as well. For the first time, Siad thought about being utterly alone. All his life, his mother had been with him, taking care of him from the time he was a baby. Siad and his mother had been through many difficult times, and they shared a bond that Siad felt could not exist between any other two people. He loved his father, but he had not always been as near to Siad as his mother was. She had always been there, and Siad could not imagine what life without her would be like, nor did he want to. He felt that he must do anything he could to ensure that she would live. As Siad tended to his mother, a Red Cross nurse came to examine her and urged Siad to

line up and receive his ration. As soon as he got the food, he rushed back to share it with his mother.

At dawn the next day, Siad's mother was still weak but, with the help of two other Somali women, Siad was able to lead her to the courtyard. As they took their places in the crowd, they were aware that there was more activity than usual. There were rumours amongst the crowd that something unusual was happening. Some were afraid and said the warlords were sending men to take the food from the compound. Others said that the food had to be bought or traded for. Siad was worried and he could sense the panic and tension in the air. When his clan had left their last campsite to come to Mogadishu, there had been fighting in the area. Innocent people had been gunned down by ruthless henchmen who were mercenaries of some warlord who claimed the land. Was this to happen again?

The terror was almost too much for him.

The Tour of Duty Begins

The roar of the airplane's engine was the only sound that could be heard as it approached its destination, Mogadishu, Somalia. Most of the soldiers were asleep, as it was late at night, but Private Flynn was lost in thought as he gazed blankly into space, contemplating the briefing he and the other soldiers had received before leaving for Somalia. Each squadron was assigned a different area of duty and was given orders for their area. Flynn's squadron was to report to a camp on the outskirts of Mogadishu. Their primary duty was to distribute food and supplies to the people there and to protect the camp from raids by the rebel forces in the area. They would have to travel to the camp by armoured vehicle, passing through some areas of the city where heavy fighting had occurred. Recently, fighting in some areas had subsided. Private Flynn hoped that they would be lucky enough to pass through these areas without too much difficulty. He was a bit scared of the dangers facing him in this strange and new land, but he knew he had duties to

perform, and he could not let his fear get the better of him. With these thoughts weighing heavily on his mind, Private Flynn drifted into a light sleep.

Suddenly, he was awakened as someone in the cockpit announced that they were about to land. Moments later the plane landed and came to a stop on the airfield. It was now ten o'clock a.m. in Somalia. The tired soldiers roused themselves and got off the plane for their first look at Somalia from the ground. The city of Mogadishu was about half a mile from here. The area of the airfield was arid and totally desolate except for a few thorny, nearly dead trees and the activity of some soldiers preparing for duty. The soldiers began to discuss what they saw.

"The land sure looks baked, doesn't it Flynn?" one of the soldiers remarked.

"It sure does, Parsons. But make no wonder! It's so hot here. We just got off the plane and already I can hardly stand the heat!" Flynn wiped the sweat from his forehead.

"I've talked to a few Americans who have been here already. They say the fighting can get really intense. I hope we get to the camp safely," Parsons said worriedly. "My folks are bound to be worried to death about me."

"Mine, too. I promised to write them once I got here. I'll have to do that once we arrive at the camp. There's the commanding officer. We must be ready to leave."

"Best of luck, Flynn. Have a safe trip," Parsons said as he did his best to hide his nervousness.

"You too, Parsons."

The commanding officer gave some last minute orders before they got into the convoy of armoured vehicles heading for the camp. As they approached Mogadishu, Flynn noticed that it was a modern city, with western and Arab style buildings. As they entered the city, however, they saw that the streets were mostly empty and some of the buildings looked as if they had been hit by mortars or rockets.

Occasionally, they heard gunshots in places where the fighting had spilled over from the harbour and other places of intense conflict to the more distanced areas. Hardly anyone dared to walk the streets. Flynn could visualize what the city must have looked like in more peaceful times, people walking the busy streets, markets bustling with activity, children playing happily, the docks filled with ships loading and unloading cargo. All this had been brought to a standstill by the war. It was disheartening to see such devastation, and he wondered how long this tour of duty would last.

Finally, the convoy reached the camp. Flynn was thankful that they had gotten through Mogadishu without any trouble. At first glance, Flynn could see a large, open courtyard with big, rusty iron gates. The people were in long lines outside this courtyard, as if waiting to get in. He then realized that this was the food compound they had been sent to protect. The convoy of trucks, jeeps, and armoured vehicles came to a stop. The next step was to make their first contact with the Somalis. This was going to be difficult. Already Flynn could see the huge mob of people buzzing and stirring about. The interpreters began to talk to the people, assuring them that no one was going to get hurt, but there was still plenty of commotion. Private Flynn knew the U.N. Peacekeeping force had a difficult task ahead of them.

CHAPTER FIVE

Hope at Last

Siad knew something important was happening. There were jeeps and strange trucks driving into the camp. In the jeeps were soldiers, and many of them were white men and women. Mohammed came running excitedly through the crowd toward Siad.

"Siad!" he exclaimed. "Have you seen the strangers? There are many white men and women amongst them. Father says they are here from a far-away place. He says he has heard they will help us keep food at our feeding station!"

Siad also noticed that several of the strange soldiers were speaking Somali, telling the people in the crowd not to panic. Everyone was excited by the sudden arrival of the soldiers. Siad believed what Mohammed had told him. If the soldiers were here to steal the food or destroy the camp, no one would be alive by now. Eventually, the soldiers reassured the people enough that they calmed down. Siad saw his mother and went to tell her what Mohammed told him. They had become separated as the neat lines of people dispersed frantically.

In all his life, Merrick Flynn had never seen such a terrible place as this camp. As the soldiers came into closer contact with the people, he could see just how desperate they were. He could think of no word to describe their paper-thin bodies. Their ribcages jutted out from their chests so that it seemed they had no flesh at all. Their limbs were as spindly as a spider's legs. He looked on in horror at the great multitude of suffering people. Some were too weak to stand. These people just laid there, as they starved and the insects tormented them. A horrible stench enveloped the whole camp, nearly choking the soldiers as they got out of their vehicles. It was the smell of filth, of rotting flesh, of starving children, of death.

He watched as frightened children cried or cowered away from them. He was surrounded by starvation, disease, and death. He felt sorry for the people of the camp, and he vowed to himself to do everything he could to help them.

Curiosity overcame Siad and he convinced his mother to allow him to go with Mohammed and approach the strangers. They walked toward a place where several jeeps were parked, and some men were speaking with a man who spoke Somali. One of the men, a soldier, asked the man who spoke Somali to help him speak to some of the people. The people were asked to remain calm and not to be afraid. They were told that the purpose of the new soldiers was good. They were here to help. Siad sensed relief amongst his people. Many in the crowd were glad to see these men. They spoke in whispers of peace and safety and, hopefully, food and water.

Later, Siad recognized the same light-haired, fair-skinned soldier and the interpreter approaching him. They stopped and spoke. The interpreter told Siad the soldier's name... Private Flynn. He also told Siad and several others that Private Flynn was from a place called Canada. Siad repeated the names "Flynn" and "Canada" and he wondered what it was like in the place where this stranger was from. He thought that Canada was very far away, since there was no food anywhere near the camp except the Unimix that the Unicef workers brought, and the soldiers said they were bringing food. There must be plenty of food and water in Canada if these soldiers could bring enough for everyone in the camp. He shyly told the men his name and then asked if this soldier had come to fight.

"No," came the soldier's answer through the

interpreter. "We do not come to fight, but to end the fighting and to bring more food." Siad thought that people from Canada must be peaceful and friendly, if they were anything like this soldier. Siad took this information to his mother. He was very excited about these strange soldiers who were bringing more food.

The next morning, the feeding station had more large vats of Unimix, and more people were doling it out. Siad spotted Private Flynn and three other Canadian peacekeepers who were clearing a way through the crowd for several Red Cross nurses. There were Unicef workers as well, helping to feed and tend to the sick, the aged and the weak.

"Where's the interpreter?" Flynn called out. "We need to tell the people to move aside." The interpreter weaved his way through the crowd, shouting instructions in Somali. Siad and Mohammed joined a group of children who were closer to the soldiers. They were fascinated with the strange language that these men spoke. Some of the children began jumping up and down, repeating strange words like "Way! Way! Clear! Clear!"

Private Flynn watched the children with

amusement. He recognized the boy named Siad. He had heard some of this boy's story from the inter-preter and several of the nurses. Although Siad was lucky to be in relatively good health compared to the people around him, it amazed him that a boy of his age already knew such pain and suffering. He had recently lost a brother and was now helping to care for his sick and grieving mother. Flynn smiled and approached the children. "Strange," he thought, "how such a forlorn and pitiful group can also be so comical."

"Siad," he said. "Hello." Flynn saw the boy's brown eyes brighten.

"Flynn," he answered, pointing at the soldier. "Flynn...hello!" Private Flynn laughed aloud as the other children in the group began chanting "Flynn...hello!"

"Looks like we have ourselves some mocking-birds," Flynn said to one of the other Canadians. He held out his hand to shake Siad's. The boy offered his

hand curiously and then smiled as Flynn clasped and shook it. Siad liked this man, this Canadian with the friendly smile.

That afternoon, Siad and his mother were eating by a shady tree. There was activity all around as soldiers and workers organized to erect several large tents similar to the ones they slept in. As he ate, Siad watched the men curiously. These tents would provide shelter. Siad was relieved to know this, because he knew his mother was tired of searching for shade every day. Siad saw two Canadian peacekeepers and an interpreter making their way toward them. They came to question Siad's mother. She was asked about her husband and eventually told that he was alive and fighting for the warlord Ali Mahdi Mohammed. Siad learned that American soldiers had recently disarmed many of these men, and they were being returned to Mogadishu. This was almost more than Siad could have hoped for! Finally, they had news of his father, and a real hope that he would return soon.

Private Flynn learned of the good news that Siad and his mother had received. He knew Siad had endured much suffering and thought that his story may have a happy ending. He was glad that he and his comrades could have such a positive effect on suffering people who needed it. Although Siad was only one child among millions of starving people in Somalia, and millions more impoverished people worldwide, it was gratifying to Flynn to know they could make a difference.

Siad looked past the crowd toward the strangers who were working to put up the tents. He saw the peacekeepers who helped to feed and care for his people. These strangers, who came as soldiers, came not to make war, but peace. Nothing could erase some of his horrible memories...nothing could bring back his brothers or the sister he had lost, but the future seemed a little brighter for Siad today.

Today, he was assured of food, medicine, and his parents. He felt safe for the first time in many months. He also felt very grateful.

CHAPTER SIX

The Tour of Duty Ends

Private Merrick Flynn awoke with a start and glanced quickly around him to get a sense of where he was. For a moment he was confused, his skin clammy and his breathing rapid. The sleeping quarters were filled with his shipmates, who were laughing and throwing various items of clothing. He noticed a damp, dirty sock laying on his chest and sat up, brushing it aside disgustedly.

"Hey, Sleeping Beauty," Parsons said with a laugh, "aren't you glad to be back in Canadian waters? Come on, let's go and watch for the shoreline."

Flynn watched as his buddies rushed off to the deck. He wondered at their antics and jovial mood. Did they dream his dreams or reflect on the past few months as he did? He was anxious to get home, but he allowed his thoughts to return to his interrupted dream, a dream that had haunted him regularly lately. He closed his eyes to summon it again. For a few minutes he was back in Somalia. Once again, he felt the hot, dry soil beneath him and saw the outlines of the Somali camp and its people, like shades of the dead, in the pale moonlight. Once again he felt the fear and uncertainty. The memory of the night the camp was attacked by young mercenaries shooting wildly from two open jeeps was still vivid, still fresh. There had been shouting, shooting, and general panic as the U.N. troops organized their defence and pursuit. Flynn's orders had been to guard the compound and protect the people of the camp. Others had left to disarm and apprehend these thugs who had come to loot and steal. The combination of

weapons and khat had led to skirmishes of this sort between rival gangs and between young gang members and U.N. peacekeepers. Situations like this were dangerous.

Training and instructions were fresh in Flynn's mind that night... he knew what he had to do. He remembered clutching his gun in his sweaty hands as he crawled along the dusty earth toward the tents containing the camp's food supply. The sound of his heart pounding became louder than the gunfire that filled the air. He thought of his family and friends. Would he ever see them again? He was terrified for his own life and the lives of those in and around the compound, but would he really shoot if he was ordered to? Could he put his training to work and shoot... to kill if necessary? It was then that he truly realized the constant danger of the situation of the peacekeepers and the inner conflict between duty and fear that tears at the soul. No amount of training could have fully prepared him for that night. As he had crouched near the tents and thought of the innocent people of the compound, who had suffered so much and whom he had worked so hard to protect these past months, he resolved that he would do whatever he was ordered to do to protect them now, even if it meant being ordered to use his rifle. Lives depended on it. His career and indeed his own life depended on it. Then, just as he was sure of himself, a horrifying thought hit home. Teenagers! These gangsters were kids! Dreaming about it, remembering it now made his stomach wrench violently. Flynn knew that they had been lucky to resolve this situation with no casualties and no bloodshed on either side. The ordeal ended seemingly as suddenly as it had begun. The young looters had been arrested and brought in with no loss of life. He found himself dashing the tears from his eyes. Thank God he'd been spared a bloody confrontation!

Slowly, Flynn stood up and stretched, rousing himself from his reverie. He reached for a glass and drank some cool water. Soon, he would be surrounded by familiar people and familiar things. Thoughts of home and family came rushing to his mind. Although it was a sobering and even a disturbing experience, Flynn knew he could never forget living amongst the people of Somalia. He could never forget the images of children laying in the dust and filth, waiting to die, nor could he forget the look of

hopelessness in their eyes. Most of all, he could not forget his feelings of inadequacy and powerlessness in the reality of that tense, bleak situation. He realized that something of his experience in Somalia would stay with him for the rest of his life. But although he felt helpless at being faced with trying to improve the lives of these people, he couldn't help but hope that he and his comrades had made a difference.

Canadian waters... Canadian soil! He would be so relieved to be back home again! Somehow, he would have to deal with these new feelings and experiences. Even though his comrades laughed and got on with their pranks, he knew they would have to, too. There would be questions to answer and emotions to sort through. They were home... but would they ever see things quite the same way? He made his way to the deck to join his friends. He resolved to make a valiant effort to pick up his spirits and resume his life. He set his jaw firmly as he stood beside Parsons and looked off into the distance... into the future.

THE PRISM AWARD WINNER

HARVEY SMITH

I am a sixteen year old grade twelve student from St. Bernard's, on the south coast of Newfoundland. I attend St. Bernard's All Grade, a facility with about 130 students. I have one sister, Janine, who is twelve years old and in grade seven. My mother and father are both teachers at a school in a neighboring community. Much of our time is taken up with classes, schedules, and courses, but we enjoy being together as a family and spending time with our large extended family whenever we can.

I'm kept very busy with schoolwork since I'm doing eight Advanced Placement (AP) courses this year. It's tough work but very rewarding. In my spare time, I enjoy listening to music, particularly modern alternative and classic rock. I also play the piano and plan to register for the royal Conservatory of Music exam for level seven piano this year. I'm also a sports fan (my favourites are baseball and hockey) and I will be cheering for the Toronto Maple Leafs again this year, no matter what happens. Needless to say, I also enjoy writing.

After I finish high school this year, I plan to attend university and pursue a career in medicine. I'm particularly interested in medical research.

I began writing Siad of Somalia as a school assignment in grade six. I wanted to write a story showing the effects that the work of the peacekeepers could have on the lives of the people they helped and protected. I had very little information on the actual situation in Somalia to begin with, except for what I read in magazine articles and saw on television. However, this was enough to instil in me a deep sympathy for the innocent victims of the conflict in Somalia, many of them children.

When my grade six teacher, Mr. Noftall, (he always asked me to mention his name in my story if it ever got published) read it, he suggested that I enter the story in a program for young writers, The Prism Awards. I did this without any real expectations. I never really thought that I, a grade six student in a school in rural Newfoundland, could win in a national program. But later, in April of 1993, I got a phone call from Lucy LaGrassa of The Kids Netword, the company responsible for the program. To my great surprise, I'd won The Prism Award in the "War and Peace" category.

At that moment, myself and my story began a long and wonderful journey that changed us both. After accepting the award, I began with an editorial instructor, Elaine Armstrong. Slowly but surely, my story grew into a book, and I became more confident in my abilities as a writer. With Elaine's guidance and the support of The Kids Netword, I did more research, including an interview with two peacekeepers who had been to Somalia, and added to the content of the story. The characters, especially Flynn, the peacekeeper, became more rounded and real. This became a story of not only how the peacekeepers, changed lives, but how their own lives were changed. It became an account of how people from entirely different backgrounds and with very different experiences can come together for a short time and then depart, each having changed forever. It also conveys a sense of hope. It imparts the belief that compassion can transcend suffering and grief, even in the direst of situations. Even though the characters in the story are entirely fictional and the situation, although based on fact to some extent, is fictional as well, I cannot help but feel in retrospect, as I hope my readers will also, that the story could quite possibly have actually happened. Although by no means perfect, Flynn is an ideal peacekeeper, with an intrinsic sense of duty, of compassion, and of humanity. He is quite a standard for our peacekeepers to live up to, but I know that all true peacekeepers, military and otherwise, have some of Private Flynn in them.

Once my book was complete, the people at The Kids Netword, and ITP Nelson went to work on the layout and publishing, and what you are reading now is the result of their hard work as well as my own. My experience with The Kids Netword has been enjoyable and exciting, as I am sure it will be for all the young authors that The Kids Netword will work with in the future.

It has been an experience I will never forget.

I hope that everyone who reads this book becomes more aware of the work of the United Nations peacekeeping forces worldwide, and that you enjoy reading it as much as I enjoyed writing it.

In conclusion, I would like to thank my family and my editorial instructor, Elaine Armstrong, whose enthusiasm and encouragement made this possible for me. Thanks also to Lucy LaGrassa and everyone at The Kids Netword, and the Department of National Defence. I would also like to thank Mr. Maurice Kelly, Mr. Leo Hynes, Mr. Mike Finn, Mr. Don Noftall, and the teachers and students of St. Berndard's All Grade.